READING MISS INGELOW. p. 54. Front.

THE

STORY OF A SUMMER;

OR,

WHAT DO YE MORE THAN OTHERS?

BY MRS. MARY E. BRADLEY.

BOSTON
D LOTHROP COMPANY
FRANKLIN AND HAWLEY STREETS

CONTENTS.

THE STORY OF A SUMMER.

CHAPTER I.

"WHO WENT TO CHURCH?"

THE Sunday morning breakfast, rather later than usual, was over, and the inmates of Mrs. Blackstone's summer boarding-house were strolling about the lawn, or chatting in groups upon the broad piazza, with the indolent air of people who have an idle day before them.

"Warm morning, Mrs. Rushmore," says young Pinckney, tossing away his cigar, as he strolls up from the lilac-walk where he has been enjoying his matutinal smoke.

"Very languid," Mrs. Rushmore responds, an equal languor in her soft voice.

"You don't attend divine worship this morn ing?" with an affected twang.

"Hardly. I seldom affect the droppings of the sanctuary in country villages."

"Sunday is the only tiresome day at the Glen," interposes Miss Fanny, with the pretty, petulant air that Mr. Pinckney finds so fascinating. "Why can't we play croquet, I wonder, or ten-pins, or something, to drive away the blues?"

"Fanny! Fanny!" Mrs. Rushmore holds up her dainty, jeweled hand with a gesture of playful reproof. "The proprieties, my dear! What will Mr. Pinckney think of your early education?"

"The better the day the better the deed," retorts the young lady. "I don't see any harm in croquet on Sunday any more than any other day. And you don't either, mamma; you needn't pretend it."

"One has to pay a certain amount of respect

to public opinion, however, and customs of society. Don't you think so, Mr. Pinckney?" Mrs. Rushmore appeals to him, and he answers gayly, —

"Oh, yes! Mrs. Grundy is omnipotent, I know; but if Miss Fanny is brave enough to defy her forms, I am brave enough to follow her lead. You have only to command, Miss Fanny; I am your obedient servant."

"And Miss Fanny, in her turn, is *my* obedient daughter," laughs Mrs. Rushmore. "And you will be so good as not to encourage her in such nonsense, Mr. Pinckney. Fanny, I shall give you a scolding as soon as you go upstairs."

"Take my advice and stay down, Miss Fanny," Mr. Pinckney suggests. And then two or three idlers join the group, and prolong the discussion with careless laugh and flippant jest, while a young girl, hardly so old as Fanny Rushmore, moves quietly away out of hearing of the conversation, whose irreverence jars painfully upon her.

"Was it Mrs. Grundy who gave the command, 'Remember the Sabbath day to keep it holy'?" she thought, as she went up to her own room. "How *can* people, with souls to be saved, be so blind and reckless? Sunday tiresome, and croquet the only thing to be desired, in the face of all this heavenly beauty!"

The picture that she looked out upon was a fair one indeed, — a green knoll, crowned with oak-trees, and sloping down to a rocky glen where the fall of a merry little brook, from stone to stone, made perpetual music; beyond, a noble river, with a chain of undulating hills stretching far away. The splendor of a July sun was upon them, bathing the hights with rosy effulgence, deepening, by contrast, the purple mist of the hollows; the river leaped and sparkled in blinding light; and the soft sward and clustering shrubbery beneath her windows and the waving oak-leaves above, were all bright with the ineffable freshness and greenness that follows the dew of a summer morning.

"The mere sense of living to-day is happiness enough," she murmured, "even, I should think, for people like the Rushmores. And for me it is praise and worship too. One need not go into temples built with hands to find God, for these purple hills show forth his glory, and the very leap and flash of this sparkling water is a psalm of rejoicing."

She drew an easy chair to the window and leaned back in a graceful, comfortable position that enabled her to enjoy the whole scene without motion. And she did enjoy it certainly, with a rapture which she believed to be altogether devotional and exalted, but which, in reality, was quite as much due to the mere satisfaction of the senses. She was keenly susceptible to pleasure or pain; she avoided involuntarily whatever jarred against her fine perceptions of beauty and delicacy; her instincts were all refined, and naturally sought expression and satisfaction in outward forms of grace and purity.

To such a temperament, religious impressions come almost spontaneously. The beautiful, the heroic, the self-sacrificing elements of Christianity appeal with a poetic charm, and the young, fervent heart clings eagerly to its ideal of divine Love. Evelyn Yale was deeply imbued with this sort of religious sentiment. She believed herself to be a sincere, humble Christian; she had lofty aspirations after missionary labor, and fancied herself quite capable of "the divine self-abnegation" (as she phrased it in her journal) of such a life. On the fly-leaf of that journal she had copied Faber's fervent lines, —

"The thought of God, above, below,
Around me and within,
Is more to me than health and wealth,
Or love of kith and kin,"

and she really believed that they expressed no more than her own heart could verify. Being in possession of both "health and wealth," and having never missed "the love of kith and kin," it was a point not so thoroughly tested as it might have been. In reality she was an earnest-minded and warm-hearted girl, having "the root of the matter in her," but being as yet far from the degree of saintliness to which she fancied herself an aspirant.

In the very matter under discussion this morning, she was unconsciously faithless to her own ideal, and proportionately as much to blame, perhaps, as the idlers on the piazza whose irreverence had so shocked her. What was she but an idler of a different sort?— lying indolently in her easy chair, feasting her senses with fair sights, and sweet sounds, and pleasant odors, while the church-bells were ringing out their summons to worship the Lord in his holy temple.

Mrs. Rushmore "did not affect the droppings of the sanctuary in country villages," and Evelyn had shrunk from the contemptuous words; but there was less difference in motive than she would have been willing to acknowledge. The same indolence of temperament disinclined both to the exertion required; the same fastidious taste made them shrink from the probable tedium of an uninteresting sermon, delivered by some unskilled country parson. Mrs. Rushmore openly avowed it; Evelyn concealed it from herself, covering up the less noble motive with an unconscious sort of affectation; "no need of seeking God in temples built with hands, while these purple hills show forth his glory!"

Which would be all very fine if in this world there were no need of example and encouragement; but what shall be done for those to whom purple hills and flashing water do not preach so eloquently as Evelyn imagined they preached to her? And these are the great majority.

Near the window, within reach of her hand, a small table stood, and upon it were arranged her favorite devotional books. A Bible and a prayer-book lay upon an embroidered mat in the center, and grouped around it were several small volumes, all of them delicately bound in Russia leather or Turkey morocco. There was a *Bogatzky*, a *Sacra Privata*, a *Thomas a-Kempis;* there was a volume of Herbert's poems, another of Hymns from Faber, and two or three of choice selections; and all of these, if you had looked through them, you would have found filled with pencilings, with pressed leaves or flowers, daintily marking some favorite passage or memorable date, with admiring or reverential personal comments, or apt quotations, neatly written upon the margins. A fragile little globe of crystal, upheld by the most aerial stem imaginable, contained one brilliant flower, a deep red rose, whose fine fragrance was perceptible above all the mingled sweetnesses of the summer morning.

This little table, a pretty thing in itself, made of costly woods, and inlaid with quaint arabesques, was Evelyn's private altar. She carried it with her, whenever she left home for any length of time, no other receptacle being deemed worthy of her precious books. Some choice flower, a spray of lilies, a cluster of heliotrope, or a rose, must always be in the little crystal vase, and the books themselves must always be in the daintiest bindings. It is to be questioned whether she did not attach an undue importance to these things,—recalling what is said of "the outside of the cup and platter,"—but no such suspicion ever entered Evelyn's mind.

She spent the morning quite to her satisfaction, enjoying dreamily for the first hour the beauty around her, and then, as the sunshine grew rather too bright and warm, she closed her blinds, and enjoyed the shadow and coolness. She read a chapter in the Bible, another in the "Imitation of Christ;" turned over the leaves of her "Changed Cross," and memorized one of the short poems, then occupied the rest of the morning in writing in her journal a rhapsody about the beauty and holiness of a Sabbath in the country, using to advantage her familiarity with Herbert and Keble for poetic illustration.

When the dressing-bell rang, she put away her journal, and arrayed herself in one of the airy, gossamer muslins which she delighted to wear. Her abundant brown hair was fastened with a pink ribbon, and a rose-bud with its leaves nestled at her throat in lieu of a brooch. Nothing fairer, sweeter, more modest and simple, than her appearance could be imagined; and more than one admiring glance dwelt upon her graceful figure and sweet girlish face, as she took her place at the dinner-table. Even young Pinckney, though wrapt in admiration of Miss Rushmore, could not help whispering to his next neighbor, —

"What a pretty little blossom it is!"

And the neighbor — an old gentleman who had not outlived his gallantry — answered loud enough for Evelyn to hear, —

"Fresh as the rose in her bosom, sir!"

Which deepened the roses in her cheeks, but at the same time sent a little flutter of pleasure to her heart. Admiration is sweet, and Evelyn was not above being pleased by it.

The usual question, "Who has been to church to-day?" arose as the bustle of taking places subsided.

"Don't all speak at once," said Mr. Pinckney in an audible "aside," nobody answering in the affirmative.

"Let me suggest an amendment to the question," put in old Dr. Gresham. "Who *didn't* go to church? I've a notion that we are all in that category to-day. For my part, I go to church — when I do go, which isn't often — for the music; and the robins and orioles have given me all the music I want to-day. Miss Yale," turning to Evelyn, "I saw you at your window after the bells had stopped ringing; your practice agrees with mine, whether your theory does or not?"

He spoke interrogatively, and Evelyn colored with a sense of embarrassment as she saw that an answer was expected from her. She was not quite willing to have it understood that her theories chimed with old Dr. Gresham's, whose free-thinking opinions had been often ventilated at the table; yet the fact remained of coincidence in practice, in the matter under discussion at least.

"I always go to church in town," she answered, with a little confusion. "In the country one doesn't feel at home; there isn't the same association, — "

"Exactly," Dr. Gresham interrupted, in the "conclusive" tone he was fond of using; "you're not so sure of the music, and the minister is apt to be a bore. I thought we should agree. Shall I help you to some salad?"

And so the question was settled apparently, and Evelyn's religious position defined, to Dr. Gresham's satisfaction at least, though it must be confessed not altogether to her own. Was this acknowledging her Master, she asked herself involuntarily, displaying the colors under which she had vowed to fight against sin, the world, and the devil? Was it not rather an actual confession that she went to the house of God only to be entertained, and stayed away when the entertainment was doubtful?

Her cheek burned with shame and confusion, and a sudden painful conviction of failure in duty broke up all the complacent serenity in which she had wrapped herself as a mantle hitherto. She longed to speak out boldly before them all, and reject Dr. Gresham's taken-for-granted conclusion. But the opportunity was lost now; he was exchanging light compliments and banter with Fanny Rushmore and her mother, and a ripple of merry talk and laughter flowed all around the table, the course of which Evelyn was not brave enough to interrupt by the very different matter that was in her thoughts. She went through her dinner mechanically, and took no part in the various topics that were discussed about her. Dr. Gresham, who had taken a fancy to her appearance and wished "to cultivate the little rose-bud," as he would have expressed it, made several vain attempts to draw her into conversation. Mrs. Maxwell and Miss Haviland, who were acquaintances in the city, kept referring to her, and others who sat near addressed her from time to time, but she gave only a divided attention to any of them, and looked so *distrait*, that Mrs. Hazleton, her aunt and her chaperon, was half provoked and half uneasy.

"What's the matter with you, Eva?" she asked a little impatiently as she followed her up to her own room. "Have you a headache, or anything? You look so disagreeably unapproachable!"

"Do I, aunt? I didn't intend to," Evelyn answered, half humbly, half wearily. "I don't think I have a headache, either."

"You seem to be in a state of uncertainty, generally," Mrs. Hazleton said rather sharply. "Dr. Gresham spoke to you twice at dinner before he could get your attention, and when he did, you answered him like a little simpleton. To Mr. Pinckney you were absolutely rude, and I wondered at Mrs. Maxwell's persistence in talking to you when you looked all the while as if you did not hear a word she said."

"I am not sure that I did," was Evelyn's reply. "At least I don't remember anything, for my thoughts were very busy with other matters."

"When you go to the dinner-table, perhaps

it would be as well to leave other matters behind," said Mrs. Hazelton. "It is not my idea of social courtesy to sit absorbed in my own thoughts, and be unable to respond even to the claims of simple politeness."

Evelyn looked up in surprise: her aunt's elaborate speeches were a sign of vexation always, and a consciousness of her own rather indifferent and unsatisfactory answers came suddenly to her. She turned to Mrs. Hazelton in quick penitence.

"I'm sorry, aunty; don't be angry with me," she said with the childish frankness that was natural to her. "I didn't mean to be rude and disagreeable, but I couldn't help it just then. I'll do better another time."

"Well, I'm sure I hope you will," Mrs. Hazleton retorted. "I don't want to be bothered with a sulky little thing who won't speak when she is spoken to even. I expected you to be the belle of the house when I brought you here; but if you go on this way, Fanny Rushmore and the Barton girls, mere chatter-boxes as they are, will carry off all the honors that ought to belong to you."

"And they are quite welcome to them, aunty; I don't want to be the belle of the house, nor any such nonsense," Evelyn cried laughingly.

"I want you to take the place that belongs to you, at any rate. You are a sensible girl, well-bred, and well-educated, and very pretty, too. And I don't choose to let you keep yourself in the back-ground. So now remember, and if you are unruly, I'll send you back to your grandmother, to be kept in town all summer."

With which threat, — not particularly alarming to Evelyn, — Mrs. Hazleton retired to her own apartments. Her husband had already donned his dressing-gown and slippers, and was taking his ease, in a masculine fashion, with his chair tipped back, his feet upon the window-sill, and a delicate wreath of cigar-smoke curling about his head. Mrs. Hazleton began to make preparations for taking her ease, in a feminine fashion. She took off her numerous ornaments, and exchanged her handsome silk dress for a loose white wrapper, arranged two or three pillows luxuriously upon the sofa, and then laid herself down, book in hand. It probably acted as a sedative, for in a few minutes her eyelids closed, and a rather sonorous breathing gave evidence that she was fast asleep.

CHAPTER II.

THE SERMON.

EVELYN, on her part, began to make arrangements of a different sort. Her floating muslin dress with its ribbons and rose-buds was taken off, and a plain walking-suit put on instead; her bonnet, gloves, and parasol were brought out from their various receptacles, and soon Evelyn stood ready to carry out the sudden resolution which she had formed, of attending the afternoon service. She did not know the hour, but it was already past three by her watch, and the village was half a mile beyond the Glen; so she concluded to start at once, and take the risk of being too early rather than too late. On the lower landing she paused and stood aside, to let a lady pass her who was coming up the stairs, and who, in answer to Evelyn's bow, looked up with a smile and a pleasant greeting.

"Are you going to walk this warm afternoon, Miss Yale, when *siestas* are the fashion of the house?"

"I never take them," Evelyn answered; "but I am not going exactly for a walk, either. I am going to church."

"Ah? but you are very early, then. The afternoon service begins at four, and it is but a little past three now. Are you going alone?"

"Yes; I know the way," said Evelyn, "but I wasn't sure of the hour, so I thought it better to start early."

"I am going too," said the lady, "and I am tempted to ask you to wait for me,—unless you would rather not have a companion?"

"Oh! indeed, I should be delighted." Evelyn colored with quick pleasure, for this was of all things what she would have wished. Mrs. Revere — Evelyn knew her name through the formal introduction at the table, by which Mrs Blackstone gave her boarders the opportunity of cultivating each other's acquaintance — was the person of all others whom she had seen in the house that she wished to know. She had never spoken with her before, for Mrs. Revere was not given to sauntering on the piazza, or lingering at the breakfast-table, and seldom made her appearance in the bowling-alley or the croquet-ground; neither did she spend her evenings, as a rule, in the parlor. So there were few opportunities of meeting her, except at the table, where her seat was not near the Hazleton party. Yet Evelyn had watched her face constantly, feeling an attraction which she could hardly define or comprehend; although indeed the face itself was worthy of study, being beautiful with an inner sort of loveliness that grew clearer and finer the longer it was dwelt upon. She did not mingle much in the general conversation of the table, yet when she spoke it was with decision as well as grace, and every one listened to her, Evelyn observed. How could they help it? she thought, for the voice was music itself, and all its graceful modulations had come to have a wonderful charm for the young girl's ear, though it was but a few days that she had been aware of them. She felt instinctively that the voice and the face were indications of a character worthy of all her love and reverence, and almost unconsciously to herself she had been hoping for some opportunity to come nearer to her, and win perhaps the recognition and response that she felt would be so sweet.

Now it had come in a moment, all unlooked-for and unexpected; just as if—she thought with a thrill of humility and gratitude—it had been sent for reward and encouragement as soon as she had turned her face toward the path of duty.

The ten minutes that she waited in the drawing-room were filled with pleasant thoughts and anticipations, mingled with new resolves toward a truer Christian life. She felt instinctively that from Mrs. Revere she would get counsel and sympathy; and this feeling was so reflected in her face when Mrs. Revere came in as to win an involuntary response in that lady's heart. She had not noticed Evelyn especially in the groups of young people who came and went in the large boarding-house; and it was a simple impulse of friendly courtesy which had led her to ask her company to church. But her first glance at the waiting face, with its expressive eyes, awakened a different and deeper interest.

The walk to the village was not in itself very attractive, a sandy foot-path, a hot sun overhead, and shade-trees in a minority, being not exactly the essential conditions of pleasantness. But Evelyn hardly felt that it was disagreeable in the charm of Mrs. Revere's presence and conversation. Not that she said a great deal, but the very first words were like an answer to Evelyn's newly-awakened consciousness.

"I was glad to see you going to church," she said, "in spite of popular opinion. If it is recognized as a duty in the city, I can't see what makes it less so in the country. On the contrary, it seems to me even more important when one is among strangers who may be influenced for good or evil by our example."

"Do you think that would have any effect?" Evelyn asked, a little anxiously and with a sense of self-reproach, remembering how she had been in the habit of considering herself only in such matters. "At the Glen, for instance, who would know or care whether I went or not?"

"No one perhaps, on this single occasion," Mrs. Revere answered. "But it would soon become known if you went habitually, from a fixed principle of duty; and the probability is that it would stimulate others to follow your example. Just as some would make it an excuse for their own neglect, that you stayed away also."

"But I am little more than a stranger here; I do not know half the people in the house by name," Evelyn urged. "My example would have very little weight."

"Everybody possesses a certain amount of influence, however," Mrs. Revere said. "We have no right to undervalue that, or overlook its possibilities of power, in any situation. You are a stranger here at present; so am I; but we shall probably be under the same roof with most of the people at the Glen for weeks and may be months to come. We shall meet at the table, and in many other ways; and of necessity, by our daily walk and conversation, make a certain impression upon each other. The silent, unconscious influence of a truly Christian life has wrought miracles of grace sometimes."

"I'm afraid I haven't thought much about other people," Evelyn acknowledged ingenuously. "I have tried to do what I thought was right,—what seemed to be right for me, at least,—but I begin to see now that that isn't the only thing to consider. I stayed away from church this morning because it was so much pleasanter to sit by the window and look at the hills and the river, and all the outside beauty. It gave me good and happy thoughts, and it didn't occur to me that I ought to go to church. I felt as well employed as if I had been there."

"Well? and then why do you go this afternoon?" asked Mrs. Revere.

"Because of something Dr. Gresham said at dinner; I dare say you didn't notice it."

"Yes, I did. He said he went to church

only for the music, and the birds at the Glen made better than he could expect to hear in the village."

"And took it for granted that I agreed with him," Evelyn added, "because he knew that I had not gone. While the truth is that I don't agree with him in the least."

"Yet you accepted the inference?"

"I know I did!" with a quick blush. "I was confused and cowardly; before I could speak he was talking of something else, and so I had not the courage to say what I really thought. But I was ashamed and unhappy; it seemed like denying *Him*, you know, to let it be believed that I only went to church to be amused. And so I made up my mind to go regularly while I stayed at the Glen, and begin this afternoon."

"That was right," said Mrs. Revere, with a smile of approval that sent a pleasant thrill to the young girl's heart. "You will define your position better by acts than words, and I shall be very glad if I can help you to keep your good resolution."

"If you will let me go with you always?" exclaimed Evelyn eagerly. "My aunt seldom goes to church herself, and I am afraid she will object to my going alone. If I am with you she will be satisfied, and for myself I am sure you will help me a good deal, if you will only talk to me and advise me a little, now and then. I have no one to tell me when I am wrong, and I make a great many mistakes," she added with real humility and a sense of shortcoming which a few hours before she would not have been capable of.

Mrs. Revere granted the request very willingly, and promised her advice whenever it was asked for, and Evelyn went into church feeling already strengthened and encouraged.

It was a little old-fashioned building, with no architectural beauty of design or finish.

The bare walls, the pulpit, the white-painted pews very sparsely filled, and the windows guiltless of Gothic arch or colored glass, were all in opposition to Evelyn's æsthetic ideas in general. Yet they did not jar upon her now, for her thoughts were lifted above the mere externals upon which she was too apt to dwell. She did notice the trailing vines that clustered round the open windows and threw wavering shadows across the aisle, as she passed up, with an involuntary recognition of their luxuriant grace and greenness; but when she took her seat and bent her head for a brief silent prayer, she felt only the sweet consciousness that "the Lord was in his holy temple," and she was permitted to worship him there.

There are certain periods in all our lives which we look back to with a thrill of remembrance, as the point where a lesson was learned, a warning apprehended, a leaf plucked from the tree of knowledge, a revelation gained, as by some heavenly inspiration, of our true selves, the needs we have been unconscious of, the sins and omissions we have not suspected, the capacities we have never put to their divinely-appointed uses. Long afterward, Evelyn Yale looked back to this peaceful Sunday afternoon as to a landmark in her earthly pilgrimage; and the rustle of green leaves about a window, with the wavering shadows across a sun-lighted floor, never failed to recall the peculiar emotions with which she listened to that simple sermon from the village pastor.

It chained her attention from the first moment; for the text was the quiet but searching question, "What do ye more than others?" and its exposition — in the very simplest language, unadorned by flower of rhetoric or grace of oratory — taught Evelyn a truth that she had never suspected before, — that she was mere idler in the Lord's vineyard, a cumberer of the ground, a butterfly sipping the sweets that others had hived, a Christian content to accept all the blessedness of Christ's love without making a single effort to glorify his name.

The minister probed his text to its deepest meaning; compared the lives of professing Christians with the people of the world, who acknowledged no higher law than that of inclination or conventionality; showed the small quantity and feeble quality of the difference that existed, in far too many instances; asserted and proved not only the possibility but the necessity of a vast difference; and concluded with an earnest and forcible appeal to the selfish and indolent Christians who were content to receive all, doing nothing in return, to arouse from their lethargy and prove themselves worthy to be followers of Christ by "doing more than others" who made no such pretense.

Whatever impression it made upon others I can not tell, but one heart, at least, was stirred to its depths, and "whereas she was blind," Evelyn Yale now saw. The revelation was no delightful one, truly: for her careless ease, it gave her disquiet; for her assured peace and happiness, it gave her doubt and distress; for her complacent satisfaction with herself, it substituted a humiliating consciousness of a life spent in self-indulgence, — innocent, graceful, amiable self-indulgence, without doubt,— but not the more to be excused for that. The hymn that followed the sermon was that old, soul-stirring, "Soldiers of the cross," and Evelyn's self-abasement culminated in the ringing lines,—

"Shall I be carried to the skies
On flowery beds of ease,
While others fought to win the prize,
And sailed through bloody seas?"

She could not join in the familiar strain,

for her voice was full of tears. Mrs. Revere's sweet and cultivated notes rang clear and thrilling above the untrained voices around her, and brought to her young companion the first sense of relief from her burden of perplexity and distress.

"She will teach me what to do; God has sent her to me," was the thought which she seized upon so eagerly. And Mrs. Revere partly comprehended it as she looked down upon the drooping, troubled face beside her — a face that stirred up memories bitter-sweet in her own heart. Years ago one that might have grown into some such likeness was hidden away from sight,—

> "Beneath the sod and the dew,
> Waiting the judgment-day."

Nobody knew what sweet hopes, that never could blossom again, were buried in the grave of that only child. Nobody knew, either, how many works of love for other young girls had been done in the name of that child by the bereaved mother. God knew, who gave the inspiration, and made her work its own reward; and from him came her intuitive apprehension of Evelyn's thoughts, her involuntary response to the unuttered appeal.

Yet they walked home almost in silence. Mrs. Revere said simply, "This was a sermon to make one think. It was like the magic mirror wherein we see ourselves as we are, and not as we seem."

"And I never saw myself before!" Evelyn exclaimed involuntarily.

"To discover that we have been following a wrong path is the first opening toward a right one," Mrs. Revere said, and then they went on silently, but with a strange sense of sympathy between them. Evelyn was too full of emotion to be able yet to put it into words; but at the gateway, before they entered the grounds of the Glen, where groups of the boarders were sauntering about, she asked half hesitatingly, but with an eagerness that her companion could not fail to recognize, —

"May I come to see you to-morrow, in your own room?"

And Mrs. Revere answered with a ready apprehension of her wish, and a cordial welcome that was balm to Evelyn's heart, —

"Indeed you may. I meant to ask you, but I am glad you thought of it yourself. Come and spend a long morning with me, and tell me all you are thinking of now."

CHAPTER III.

MISS INGELOW'S POETRY.

"ARE you ready for tea, Eva?"

Mrs. Hazleton came into her niece's room, very handsome in her evening dress and carefully-arranged hair, and took a critical survey of the young lady whom she wished to see "the belle of the house." Evelyn had somewhat hastily rearrayed herself in the same muslin which she wore at dinner, and her aunt was slightly contemptuous.

"One would think you had nothing else to wear, Eva. Why couldn't you put on something nicer for Sunday evening, when everybody dresses so much?"

"It was the first thing I saw, aunty, and so I

took it. I have been to church, and I was a little hurried."

"To church this hot afternoon! and without consulting me? All alone, too, I suppose. Really, Evelyn," and Mrs. Hazleton grew elaborate, "I think that religion might possibly be compatible with a little observance of propriety, to say nothing of deference to your elders."

"I did not go alone, aunt, though I don't think there would have been any impropriety if I had," Evelyn answered with a certain quiet firmness that she could display on occasion. "I intend to go regularly after this to both services: and Mrs. Revere is so kind as to let me be her companion. I went with her to-day."

"Mrs. Revere? Oh, indeed!" Mrs. Hazleton's tone of displeasure changed to a curious blending of surprise and satisfaction, mingled with a little personal pique. She was better aware than Evelyn of Mrs. Revere's social standing, several grades higher than her own, and had made some rather ineffectual advances toward cultivating an acquaintance. It was a little provoking that Evelyn should accomplish so easily what she had failed in; yet being "all in the family," as she remembered, the end to be gained was the same. So she put aside her own sense of failure in her satisfaction at Evelyn's success, and forbore to make any objections to her intended line of conduct.

"If Mrs. Revere goes with you, of course it will be perfectly proper," she said amicably. "But there is one thing I beg of you, Eva: don't be so disagreeably pious that you can't take part in the natural diversions and amusements that belong to your age. I can't bear to see young people set themselves up as examples of goodness. They only succeed in making themselves ridiculous."

"I shan't try to do anything so impossible," was Evelyn's answer, half humble, half proud. She knew she was no "example of goodness," and she equally rejected the idea that she could be ridiculous in any circumstances.

"I want you to stay down after tea," Mrs. Hazleton continued, "and make yourself agreeable. It is not a religious duty to shut yourself up because it is Sunday. I wish you had put on that rose-colored grenadine, instead of this insignificant little muslin; but it is too late to change now — there is the last bell."

"Shall I do what she wants?" Evelyn asked herself as they went down together. "I did mean to spend the evening alone, to think, and pray, and try to find out how to live differently and better. But that is the sort of thing I have done all along,— separated myself from others,— not tried to do anything for them. What *can* I do?"

"Try in the first place to please your aunt,

whenever you can without wrong," some inner voice answered.

And she accepted it simply, resolving to watch and pray that it might lead her into no temptation.

There were a great many elegant toilets around the tea-table that evening; shimmering silks, and gauzy, brilliant tissues, and sparkle of costly ornaments; but the "little rosebud," in spite of her simplicity, was still the attraction to Dr. Gresham. He addressed himself to her as soon as she appeared, asking her opinion about a book of poems which had recently come across the water for American appreciation. And as Evelyn happened to be familiar with it, and the topic was one which brought out her best conversational ability, she did herself justice, to her aunt's satisfaction. Dr. Gresham was also a person of note in her eyes, and being so much older than Evelyn, there could be no impropriety in her receiving so much of his attention; while on the other hand it conferred a certain distinction upon her that she should be singled out for it, from all the other young ladies.

Mrs. Hazleton had an eye for all possible worldly advantages; Evelyn was too really simple-hearted to consider them at all. But she enjoyed this talk about books with the well-read and well-bred gentleman — who was old enough to be her father, and so put her at her ease — very much indeed. All the more because her friend Mrs. Revere took part in it with equal interest. She had not seen the volume, but she had read and admired some extracts floating through the papers; and Evelyn was very glad of the opportunity to offer her the book.

"Did you really bring it with you?" Dr. Gresham asked, looking pleased. "Now, that will give you an opportunity, Miss Yale, to confer a great enjoyment upon me. I am sure you read aloud charmingly, and there is nothing I would like so well as to hear you read some of those poems."

"Oh, indeed!" Evelyn exclaimed hastily, "you are very much mistaken, Dr. Gresham. You would not like it at all,—I should only spoil the poems for you."

She was confused by the unexpected request and the attention it drew upon her, and her face grew warm with the nervous dread that he would persist in it. The soft pink flush that mantled cheek and throat so suddenly was far from unbecoming; and partly from a mischievous enjoyment of her embarrassment, as well as a real wish to hear her read, Dr. Gresham insisted upon her obliging him.

"I am an old man, Miss Yale, without a great many pleasures left me to enjoy; and you are too kind-hearted, I am sure, to deny me one that you can so easily bestow."

"But I can't—I really can't read alone—

if you only heard me once, you would believe me," was Evelyn's distressed answer. But the doctor retorted that he was a doubting Thomas, and nothing but auricular evidence would satisfy him; and Mrs. Hazleton interposed,—

"What nonsense you are talking, Evelyn! Indeed, Dr. Gresham, you need not believe a word of it; she reads delightfully." Which was a statement not at all borne out by her actual knowledge, since she had certainly never tested her niece's accomplishments in that line. She had a complacent belief, however, in Evelyn's general cleverness, and was determined not to let such an opportunity for displaying it pass by. Evelyn found herself in a position most embarrassing to a sensitive nature. Mr. Pinckney—always eager for anything new—was adding his entreaty; Fanny Rushmore put in sarcastically,—

"We are all hanging upon your lips, Miss Yale!"

Mrs. Maxwell said good-naturedly, "Come, Eva, you might as well yield gracefully." And two or three more of the circle about her joined in the chorus, not because they cared any thing about it, but just because people are so apt to "follow my leader." So she had the equally unpleasant alternative of appearing selfishly disobliging, or being made conspicuous; perhaps to be laughed at and criticised afterwards by the very ones who were compelling her to yield against her protest.

It may seem a trifling matter, hardly worth her hesitation, simply to have read aloud a poem to a few hearers. But the reader being a timid young girl, and the audience composed of such mixed elements, it was no small trial of her courage. There was one person at the table who understood it, and it was something in Mrs. Revere's sympathetic glance that nerved Evelyn to a decision.

"I am afraid you will repent of asking me,"

— she turned to Dr. Gresham with a smile — "but if you won't take warning, why you must take the consequences."

"With all my heart!" was the gallant reply. "And I'll take them immediately, if you please, Miss Yale. This is the very hour for poetry and sentiment. Let us adjourn to the west piazza, and meet Miss Ingelow — not by moonlight alone, but by sunset in the best of company."

So Evelyn resigned herself to her fate, and went up for the book. When she came down, they were all gathered in the west piazza, so called, though it was more like a summer-house. It was crescent-shaped, encircled with a close hedge of arbor-vitæ kept even with the rails, and overhung by two beautiful mountain-ash trees. A rustic table made of branches of trees cunningly twisted together, and chairs and benches of the same fashion, gave a summer-house aspect to the pretty spot; and these comforts, together with the glorious view of the river and the distant hills which it commanded, made the west piazza a very favorite resort. The little rustic table often held a welcome little collation of fruit and cake and ice-cream provided for the young ladies by their gentlemen admirers; and the echo of merry voices, laughter and singing rang there every evening till late in the summer night.

It was something new to find all the talkative groups sitting silent, waiting on the voice of one young girl; rather ridiculous, too, as some of them thought; and Evelyn instinctively felt their thought, not with a reassuring effect.

"If only some one else would read?" she said with an appealing glance to Mrs. Revere, "It is a shame to spoil Jean Ingelow."

"You'll not spoil her." Mrs. Revere smiled encouragingly, as she made a place for Evelyn by herself. And so with an effort of self-control, and a shrinking from the sound of her own voice, which only Mrs. Revere appreciated, Evelyn began to read. The poem she chose first was that wonderful "High-Tide." The tragic story, the flowing, musical rhythm, the quaint simplicity, the ineffable pathos and melody of the whole poem, chained attention from the first; and though Evelyn's voice was somewhat low and tremulous in the beginning, it steadied itself unconsciously very soon. She had the sympathy of her listeners, which put her at ease, and she possessed the essential quality of a good reader, the power to render feelingly what she keenly felt herself.

The "High Tide" was a perfect success, and a murmur of voices rose around her when she had finished. "How charming!" "How pathetic!" "What melodious music! and how sweetly you have read it!" "Do read something else, Miss Yale!"

"Am I not justified?" said Dr. Gresham

graciously. "I hope you are all duly grateful to me for presenting this young debutante, so unconscious of her own powers."

"She knew that would highten the effect," said Mrs. Maxwell playfully. "Read something else, Evelyn; you've no sort of excuse now."

"May I read my own favorite?" asked Evelyn, with a sudden impulse. "It is long, and it isn't in rhyme, and perhaps you will not like it. But *I* think it is the noblest poem in the book; and it suits for Sunday reading."

"Read it then by all means," said Mrs. Revere quickly. The others assented, and though Evelyn caught Fanny Rushmore's sarcastic whisper to Mr. Pinckney, "Blank verse, and pious! Why not have Young's Night Thoughts?" she did not shrink from her purpose.

"*Brothers, and a Sermon,*" was the name of the poem, and those who are familiar with it will need no comment here upon its matchless fervor and tenderness. Evelyn had read it to herself over and over again with ever new admiration; she knew how to read it effectively, in spite of its frequent changes of tone, and even as her own heart had thrilled to the passionate pleading of the grand old preacher, so her rapt and earnest utterance of his wonderful "sermon," impressed vividly the hearts of her listeners. Mrs. Revere's face grew paler and more intense as she listened; tears gathered in Dr. Gresham's eyes, which he was not ashamed to wipe away; even Fanny Rushmore sat eager, with lips parted, and a dawn of deeper feeling in her look than she was often suspected of possessing. It filled Evelyn with a sort of inspiration: she forgot all self-consciousness, and for the time was imbued only with the one absorbing desire of the preacher — that *her* hearers, too, might open the door, and answer Him who saith, "I stand and knock."

Her girlish voice grew deep with some inard power, as she read:

"O Lord, our Lord,
How great is thy compassion! Come, good Lord,
For we will open. Come this night, good Lord,
Stand at the door and knock.

"And is this all?
Trouble, old age, and simpleness, and sin —
This all? It might be all some other night.
But this night, if a voice said 'Give account;
Whom hast thou with thee?' then must I reply,
Young manhood have I, beautiful youth and strength
Rich with all treasure drawn up from the crypt
Where lies the learning of the ancient world
Brave with all thoughts that poets fling upon
This strand of life as drift-weed after storms;
Doubtless familiar with Thy mountain-heads,
And the dread purity of Alpine snows;
Doubtless familiar with Thy works concealed
For ages from mankind — outlying worlds
And many-mooned spheres — and Thy great store
Of stars, more thick than mealy dust which here
Powders the pale leaves of auriculas.

"This do I know, but, Lord, I know not more;
Not more concerning them. Concerning thee,
I know Thy bounty; where Thou givest much,
Standing without, if any call Thee in
Thou givest more. Speak then, O rich and strong,
Open, O happy young, ere yet the hand
Of Him that knocks, wearied at last, forbear,
The patient foot its thankless quest refrain,
The wounded heart for evermore withdraw."

There was a breathless pause for a minute when she closed the book. No one asked for any thing more, with an instinctive sympathy of feeling that the effect of this should not be marred. Many thoughts were striving in the hearts of this group; thoughts new and awful to some, solemn and sweet to others,— for there were others there besides the young reader, who had heard the voice of Him who has said, through so many patient, thankless years, "I stand at the door and knock." Their ears had grown dull to it, perhaps they had forgotten some of the joy with which they "opened the door" at first, to welcome Him in; they had neglected to cherish the heavenly visitor, and fallen away from their first love; now their world-hardened hearts grew tender with quick remorse, touched by the unexpected warning.

Others — like Dr. Gresham's, Pinckney's, Fanny Rushmore's — were roused from the careless ease which had no consciousness of any thing lacking. Was there not something here that concerned them? And it was not so easy to shake off the impression of that thrilling voice, calling so vainly to them through all these years.

Somebody suggested music presently. The piano stood near the wide window which opened on the west piazza, and Mrs. Revere went in quietly, and began to play. She was known to be a fine musician, and her rendering of Chopin and Mendelssohn was a rare enjoyment. But she played no symphonies or sonatas to-night. A few simple chords that woke a familiar strain; then her beautiful, tender voice in the well-known hymn —

> "Jesus and shall it ever be,
> A mortal man ashamed of thee?"

Evelyn could not stay outside, sweet as it was in the dewy twilight. She came in and stood by the piano, where she could see as well as hear the singer. Dr. Gresham followed her presently.

"My mother used to sing that when I was a child," he said, when the hymn was ended. "I have not heard it in many years, but it wakes up memory now. She sang it as you do, with an enthusiasm, a sense of exaltation, that used to thrill me, though I did not understand it then any more than I do now."

"But it is so easily understood," Mrs. Revere said simply. "How can one help being exalted with the idea that Christ, the Son of God, is his friend?"

"It is a beautiful *idea,*" said Dr. Gresham, with a slight emphasis on the word.

"It is more than that; it is a saving truth," she answered. "Your mother knew it, and so do I."

"My mother was a good woman. If she had lived longer, she might have inspired me with her faith. There is something attractive in these childhood creeds, I grant you, Mrs. Revere, but when the mind wakes up to reason, there is no ground left for them to stand on."

"Not to the wise and prudent," she murmured, more to herself than in answer to him. She would not argue the question with Dr. Gresham — now at least, for the rest were coming in from the piazza, and another hymn was asked for. She sang "Rock of Ages," and very soon the sweet strain was swelled with other voices than her own. Then more hymns — the old familiar words to the old familiar tunes, that held some sacred or tender association for almost every one there — were sung in the deepening twilight. And so the Sunday evening passed away, more like a Sabbath than it was wont to be at the Glen. "Quite like a little prayer-meeting," Mrs. Hazleton said with a slight yawn, as she kissed Evelyn good-night. "Still, it was very pleasant and suitable, and you really made quite an impression with your reading, Eva. It is worth while being obliging and complaisant, you see."

CHAPTER IV.

VISIT TO MRS. REVERE.

EVELYN anticipated her visit to Mrs. Revere with eager interest. Her newly-awakened consciousness needed direction, and she felt sure that her friend could advise and direct, and utilize, so to speak, her desire to render a more faithful and self-denying service.

She was not disappointed in this belief. Mrs. Revere's life had been very rich in experience; she had been over the whole ground of Evelyn's difficulty, and no one was better calculated to guide and sympathize. They were very happy hours that Evelyn spent in Mrs. Revere's room that Monday morning;

not merely in earnest conversation, but in a little practical work already. There was a small heap of white bundles lying upon a table, and while she talked, Mrs. Revere opened one of these, and began sewing up a seam in what appeared to be a sort of doll's night-gown. Evelyn watched her curiously for a while; at last she yielded to the impulse to ask what the work was.

"You can't be really making doll's clothes?" she said laughingly.

"Why not?" Mrs. Revere smiled. "I have dressed a great many dolls, and expect to dress a great many more, if I shall live."

"But you have no children."

"There are a great many in the world, however, and I have found it easy to dispose of all my dolls."

Evelyn colored as a new light broke upon her. "You give them away to poor children!" she exclaimed. "Now why did *I* never think of doing such things? I have had time enough, and money enough, and how many poor little things I might have made happy, if I had only thought of it!"

"You remember Hood's poem of 'The Lady's Dream?'" asked Mrs. Revere. "He never wrote anything truer than the closing lines:

'Evil is wrought by want of thought,
As well as want of feeling.'"

"And how much I must have wrought!" Evelyn cried, with genuine regret. "I have only thought of myself all my life, I am afraid. And yet I didn't know,—I never meant to be so selfish. If any body had come to me in trouble, I should have been sorry, and tried to help. No one ever did though."

"But the world is full of trouble, my dear. It lies before our eyes in one shape or another all the while; we leave it behind us in the old place, and we meet it again in the new. The wonder is how any one can avoid seeing it."

"I suppose I have gone through the world with my eyes shut," Evelyn answered humbly. "If you will help me to open them, I shall be very thankful. And if you will let me help you now with your doll's clothes?"

"I did not say they were doll's clothes," Mrs. Revere returned, with a smile. "Perhaps you will enjoy the work more if I tell you that they are intended for flesh-and-blood dolls."

"They are too little!" Evelyn exclaimed. "No human child could wear such a garment as that."

Mrs. Revere held up the little slip, and laughed herself at its tiny proportions. "But nevertheless," she said, "it is quite large enough for the baby who will wear it. Have you ever walked through that little settlement below the hill, near the railroad?"

No, Evelyn acknowledged she never had. There were too many dirty children, too many strings of wet clothes, too much shabbiness and poverty to tempt her near it. She had wished sometimes, as she stood upon the green hill overlooking the river, that all those shabby little tenements could be blotted out of the landscape; they spoiled its beauty.

"They give shelter to twenty or thirty families," said Mrs. Revere, "who would be homeless if you had your wish. In one of them there are two little new-born children, whose father was killed on the railroad a month ago; their mother lies ill and helpless with nobody to care for her, and the poor little twins found nothing ready for them when they came into the world."

"And *you* are making clothes for them!" Evelyn exclaimed. "What little, *little*, creatures they must be! May I really help you? I can sew very nicely, indeed."

"Indeed, I shall be very glad of your help. The twins need their little garments quite as much as if they were bigger, and I want to finish them as soon as possible."

"I will run and fetch my thimble," said Evelyn eagerly. "May I sit with you and sew?"

"Certainly you may."

And Evelyn flew up to her own room in a happy excitement, to get her work-box. Mrs. Hazleton met her in the hall.

"Where are you, Eva?"

"Down stairs with Mrs. Revere. And oh, aunt, there are two little babies down by the railroad—twins, with nothing to wear; and she is going to let me help her make some clothes for them!"

Evelyn's eyes sparkled with her eager interest; and her aunt, who had just accepted an invitation to drive with Mrs. Maxwell, was rather glad that she had found something to amuse her.

"If you want any thing to make up," she said graciously, "there is a piece of white cross-bar in my trunk that you may have. I bought it for a dressing-wrapper, but it is rather coarse, and I shan't use it. It will make slips for your twins."

"Oh, thank you!" Evelyn gave her a rapturous kiss, and darted off to get her muslin. Mrs. Hazleton went away for her drive in all the better humor, and her niece was soon again in Mrs. Revere's room with her work-box and the new contribution to the twins' ward robe, which proved to be highly acceptable. There was enough of it to make four nice dresses for them, and Mrs. Revere cut them out at once, while Evelyn took up the little night-gown and finished it.

It was one of the happiest mornings she had ever spent. The hours flew by, the little garments grew under the busy hands, and Evelyn felt as if she was growing too, in the sunshine of her friend's ripe experience. If she had never seen her again the influence of this morning would still have remained; she could never have gone back again to the old indolent, self-indulgent manner of life. Her eyes were opened now, her conscience aroused, and henceforth if she lived to herself only it was willfulness not ignorance. Happily for her, the intercourse which had proved so beneficial in its beginning was likely to continue. Mrs. Revere saw in the young girl possibilities of a beautiful Christian development, and she was not one to neglect any opportunity for doing herself, or helping others to do, her Master's work.

"You would not like to go with me this afternoon, to carry these little garments, would you?" she asked, when the dressing-bell rang, and two of the night-gowns were folded up, finished.

"Indeed I would, if you would let me!" was Evelyn's ready answer.

"But they are shabby little houses; there

are bad smells, and dirty children, and possibly pigs, to be encountered!"

"I don't care. If you are not afraid of the pigs, why should I be?"

"What will your aunt say?"

"I don't think she will make any objections if I am with you," said Evelyn simply.

"I will ask her myself to allow you," Mrs. Revere promised, being sufficiently clear-sighted to guess that Mrs. Hazleton would be flattered by the request. Evelyn knew very well that she would yield a gracious consent to any thing Mrs. Revere asked, though otherwise she would have been shocked at the idea of her niece being seen in such places. And the result proved that she was not mistaken. Down-stairs, to Mrs. Revere, Mrs. Hazleton said in her most affable manner:

"Certainly Evelyn may accompany you; I am very happy to allow her. When she is with you I can not have any anxiety about her."

But up-stairs, to her niece, Mrs. Hazleton said, rather fretfully:

"I should think you might be contented with doing the work, Eva, without wanting to poke about in those dirty little holes; such hot weather, too! I only hope you won't bring home the small-pox, or something."

"Don't be afraid, aunty; Mrs. Revere knows all about the place. She wouldn't take me if there was any danger," Evelyn answered cheerfully.

"People have very queer tastes," Mrs. Hazleton continued. "I believe in being charitable; I am always willing to give what I can, but I don't see any good in going about these Irish tenements, and exposing yourself to all sorts of disagreeable things. If it was any body but Mrs. Revere, you shouldn't go one step."

Which Evelyn knew very well beforehand. As it was Mrs. Revere, however, she went, and was certainly none the worse for going. She saw the twins, and their mother, — a poor young creature not many years older than Evelyn herself, yet burdened with the sorrow of widowhood, the cares of maternity, and the bitter anxieties of poverty. The babies were like dolls, the tiniest creatures she had ever seen in her life. She took one of them in her hands, and tried to dress it in the clean white slips she had brought; but the little soft head that rolled about so helplessly frightened her.

"I shall break its neck; I can't do it," she said, half laughing, half ashamed. And Mrs. Revere, who had already robed the other child, with her gentle, skillful hands, took it from her, and showed her how to support the uncertain little head, and the back that had no bone in it yet, to signify. They looked very pretty and winsome after they were dressed; and the young mother was overflowing with gratitude.

"I had no heart at all to do a thing, she said to Evelyn, "even if I'd had any thing to do with. When my man was killed, I just wanted to die myself as quick as I could. And I thought I would die when the babies came, and it would all be over. But I didn't, and the little things were naked in the world; and only for this lady—God bless her!—I don't know what would have become of us."

Evelyn looked at her friend; she could not speak, for her eyes were full of tears, her heart of loving admiration. Mrs. Revere smoothed softly the little head that lay in her lap.

"You have something to live for now," she said cheerfully to the mother. "Here are two dear little lives to work for; two precious little souls to watch over, and keep out of evil. They have a heavenly Father, you know, and he will not forsake you or them, if you will only trust him, and obey him, and bring up your children to love him."

"I'll try, indeed I will!" was the mother's tearful answer. And Evelyn could guess at the ministry of love that had been performed here. There was a cradle beside the bed, new and neat, with all its little accompaniments; and the mother's garments, as well as the twins', had evidently been supplied by Mrs. Revere. But more than all this, even, was the heavenly charity which had not merely relieved physical wants, but had given tender sympathy, wise consolation, and gentle leading toward the Fountain of all comfort.

It was a lovely walk home in the evening dew and coolness. They stood upon "the Green" a sort of village common on an elevation above the river, and watched the exquisite tints in sky and water which the sunset had left behind. A rosy cloud hung over the extreme end of Croton Point, and was reflected with equal glow in the bright river beneath; Hook Mountain stood out bold in a royal mantle of purple against a golden background and all the graceful Highland range with the far away, misty hills behind, took on new beauty in the changeful splendor of the clouds.

The steamboats were coming in, their bright streamers floating on the breeze, and a long white wake glittering behind them. On the Green, groups of people walked about, or sat on the rocks watching the boats. They were village people with their children, mostly; but some were from the boarding-houses, waiting the arrival of husbands and brothers who went to their daily occupations in the city, and came back again to country coolness and quiet in the evening.

"Here comes the Sleepy Hollow," Evelyn cried presently. "She will be the first boat in to-night, and uncle and Mr. Maxwell will be on board. Can't we wait to meet them? You are not in a hurry to dress for tea?"

"No indeed," Mrs. Revere answered readily. "I am glad of an excuse to stay here always; this view is so beautiful. There comes Mrs. Maxwell now, and Miss Haviland is with her."

"She always comes to meet her husband," said Evelyn. "I see her tripping down those steps in the terrace every evening. They are right under my window, you know, and I like to watch her. She goes down that steep hill with such a pretty, flying step, as if she was so eager to get there and meet her husband."

"She is very fond of him," was Mrs. Revere's assenting comment.

"Here come the little Bartons with their nurse, to meet their papa," cried Evelyn. "I like to see children do that. Oh, and there are the little Cubans! What pretty names they have, Manuelo and Dolorita De gardo! And what pretty sparkling faces!"

She was quite unconscious that her own was equally "pretty and sparkling" in her happy excitement, born of the new delight of doing good. Mrs. Revere watched her, and listened to her girlish flow of talk, with a sense of something very sweet in it not unmingled with sadness. Widowed and childless, she stood isolated from the dearest relations of life, and notwithstanding her elevated christian character, which accepted her lot and ennobled it, she could not help feeling this isolation very keenly at times. Her heart had often ached with loneliness when she saw other mothers with their daughters around them; but she had never envied any mother her treasures, or singled out any child with the secret wish that she could call it her own. Never until to-day; but now she looked at the fresh young face beside her, knowing it to be fitly companioned with an earnest, pure, reverent nature, and wished that Evelyn Yale could be to her as a daughter.

Unconscious of her friend's thoughts, Evelyn

ARRIVAL OF THE SLEEPY HOLLOW.

stood enjoying the scene around her, and the remembrance of the one she had left behind. The tiny, comical twin babies and their patient mother mingled oddly and yet pleasantly with the bright little Cuban children in dark ringlets and scarlet ribbons; with Mrs. Maxwell and Miss Haviland in their pretty evening dresses; with all the throng, and chatter, and gayety that was increasing on the Green; yet she seemed to see the one picture as plainly as the other, and enjoyed the pleasantness of both, though it had such opposite sources.

The Sleepy Hollow had made her landing, and the passengers were scattering to their different destinations; some going up the steep main-street into the village, others rolling off in carriages and "democrats," and a few — chiefly the gentleman-boarders from the Glen — climbing the winding and irregular path among the rocks that led up to the Green.

"There is Dr. Gresham!" Evelyn exclaimed

suddenly. "He must have been to the city to-day, but he doesn't go generally."

"Your uncle is following him up the rocks," said Mrs. Revere.

"And there's my husband!" cried Mrs. Maxwell merrily, waving her scented handkerchief as another head rose in sight.

"'I see them on their winding way!"' sang Miss Haviland. "Here comes my brother with Mr. Delgardo. Dolorita, come and meet your father."

The dark-eyed little gypsy shook back her long curls, and ran forward, holding Miss Haviland's hand, to the brow of the hill. The rest followed more leisurely, Evelyn's eye singling out — she did not ask herself why — Dr Gresham's large figure, as he picked his way up the difficult path. Suddenly she gave a cry, and seized Mrs. Revere's arm.

"Dr. Gresham has stumbled on the rocks; he is falling!"

Her cry was echoed by a scream from the children, who stood nearer the edge of the cliff; and a sudden confusion and clamor arose, people hurrying to the place, and every body asking every body else what was the matter. Mrs. Revere asked no questions; but she and Evelyn went forward with swift steps, and reached the rocky ledge just in time to see a group of gentlemen trying to raise the doctor into a sitting position. His face was white, his head drooped on one side in a lifeless manner.

"He is badly hurt, I am afraid," Mr. Maxwell said; "it was a very awkward fall. Annie!"—to his wife who was looking down, horror-stricken—"have you got any smelling-salts about you? He has fainted with the pain. I think he has broken his leg."

"Oh, I haven't a thing; I'm sorry!" Mrs. Maxwell exclaimed helplessly.

"I have some hartshorn." It was Mrs. Revere's quiet voice, and the next minute she was kneeling beside the fainting man, applying the pungent remedy to his nostrils. It roused him from the stupor of pain.

"My leg—I have broken it!" he murmured with an effort. "I can't stir."

"Don't try to," said Mrs. Revere gently. There are plenty here to help you; the gentlemen will get a litter."

And acting on her suggestion, too or three started off with all speed to the cottages beyond, to see what could be procured, while another hurried on to the village to find a doctor. Evelyn stood mute with keen sympathy; Mrs. Revere supported the drooping head until Mr. Hazleton and Mr. Maxwell came back with a shutter and some blankets hastily folded upon it; and her womanly hands were as helpful as the stronger arms of the men, in laying the wounded man tenderly and carefully upon it.

CHAPTER V.

DR. GRESHAM'S OPINION.

"A COMPOUND fracture of the thigh" was the result of the surgeon's investigation, "and it was impossible to tell how long he might be helpless. For weeks, certainly, and perhaps for months. A difficult case to handle!"

There was a great deal of excitement about it at the Glen. "Those dreadful rocks!" cried little Mrs. Maxwell, with a shiver. "I have begged Charlie never to climb up them again. It is a great deal better to go around through the village."

"Up that hill Difficulty that they call Main Street?" asked Mr. Hazleton. "Never, for me. The rocks are well enough, if one is only a little careful of one's footing. I can't think what the doctor was about to let himself fall."

"How dull it will be for him, poor doctor!" said Mrs. Rushmore, with languid sympathy; "shut up with a broken limb all this bright summer weather."

"You ladies will have a good opportunity to show yourselves ministering angels," laughed Mr. Pinckney. "What is it the poet says—

"'When pain and anguish wring the brow,
A ministering angel thou!'"

"Ah, that's poetry," said Fanny Rushmore, "but the prose of it isn't so nice. I haven't any vocation for a sick-room; I tumble the medicine-bottles down, my dress rustles, and my shoes creak, in spite of me; I am out of my element altogether, and every body is glad to be rid of me."

"Fanny, you will make Mr. Pinckney believe you, if you keep on in that strain," her mother interposed.

"Well, so he may!" and the young lady shrugged her pretty shoulders. "I'm no sort of use when any one is sick, mamma; you know it. It only makes me blue to see them, and so I keep out of the way. I'm excessively sorry for poor Dr. Gresham, but I've no idea of offering myself for his nurse!"

"We shall miss him very much," said Clara Barton. "He was worth all the rest of you gentlemen at croquet, or for a drive or a picnic. He was always getting up something pleasant to amuse us; it's just too provoking that he should have got that fall!"

A rather selfish view of the case, Evelyn could not help thinking, as she sat silent amidst the flow of conversation about her. It was nevertheless the one which received most consideration amongst the gay young people at the Glen. The doctor was entertaining and obliging; he planned new amusements for them; he was always at their service when he was wanted; they "missed him" for this, and after the first feeling of commiseration, and the first formal visits of condolence, Dr. Gresham dropped out of their thoughts pretty generally, as being no longer available for the grand object of life,—amusement.

There were honorable exceptions, of course. Mrs. Maxwell made a duty of going up every few days to inquire of his attendant how the doctor was progressing. Occasionally she went in, and brightened the room for a few minutes with her pretty looks and cheerful words. There were others who did as much; but after all, his long confinement would have been a dreary one indeed, except for Evelyn and Mrs. Revere.

The first time that he was allowed to see visitors, after the limb had been set, and the crisis of fever passed, he asked particularly for them. They came in, Mrs. Revere cheerful, serene, encouraging as always, the very ideal of a "ministering angel" in a sick-room; Evelyn full of eager sympathy. His eyes brightened at the sight of "the little rose-bud," and the visit cheered him so much as to make a visible improvement. He begged that it might be repeated; and so it grew into a daily thing, by and by. They brought their sewing, sometimes, and completed the twins' wardrobe under the doctor's supervision; he taking a hearty interest in its progress, and evincing as much practically by a generous donation for the poor mother.

Often they read to him. Evelyn's copy of Jean Ingelow lay on his table permanently, and she was called upon for her favorite Brothers, and a Sermon" more than once. He was never weary of her voice; it soothed his pain and restlessness more effectually than any thing; and knowing this, she never suffered him to see that she was weary of reading, though it was often a visible truth.

The windows of his room overlooked the croquet-lawn. The merry voices of the players floated up to her ears, and she had at times a wistful longing to join them. She was young, and far from indifferent to the companionship of her mates, or the innocent pleasures which they enjoyed. They were glad to have her too; for she had made herself liked generally in the house, and there was seldom any amusement proposed in which she was not invited to take part. She accepted the invitation when she could, but she had very frequently to make the choice between duty and inclination; and she would not give up her sewing for some poor woman who needed the unfinished garments, her reading to the invalid, or her visits to the cottages with Mrs. Revere, for the sake of a drive, a boating excursion, or a game of croquet.

Mrs. Hazleton fretted and scolded at first; declared it was absurd to take up a round of pious duties in the summer-time, when one came to the country to amuse one's self, and threatened Evelyn more than once that she should be sent back to her grandmother. But after all, she secretly respected her niece all the more for her quiet persistence in the line of conduct she had marked out for herself. And after a while she ceased to oppose her; she found agreeable companions among the lady-boarders, and was content to let her niece find hers chiefly with Mrs. Revere.

So the summer days sped on, and the lesson which Evelyn had learned from the good minister's sermon struck its roots deeper into her heart, and blossomed out in honest purpose and self-denying practice. She did not know the good that she was doing, but she at least kept her eyes open for opportunities, and tried to neglect none that occurred. She had no suspicion of the change that she was working gradually in Dr. Gresham's opinions. Her gentle services to him, at the sacrifice of so many of her natural enjoyments, and her simple yet steadfast faith and piety, had more influence upon him than even Mrs. Revere's Christian conduct and profession.

"Women like you" — he spoke his thought alone to her once, when Evelyn was not there — "fall back upon religion naturally, as an outlet for other feelings which are checked. You are widowed, you are childless, you have suffered the loss of all your precious things; and with your deep, loving nature, you cannot enjoy a life empty of love. So you reach your arms out to heaven, and fill your heart with a spiritual worship. I understand the necessity and I watch its development with a certain admiration. But it does not convince me that religion is the grand, universal good. This is what I would have told you a month ago."

"Well, and now?" asked Mrs. Revere, smiling, yet with a sudden, secret hope upspringing.

"Now, I will tell you that your little friend, Miss Yale, has given me some different ideas. She is a good little Christian, is she not?"

"The sincerest, the humblest that I know," said Mrs. Revere, warmly.

"So it seems to me. She does not obtrude herself religiously, but her sweet little life is a more convincing sermon to me than I ever heard in a pulpit. She is very young and very pretty; life shows its cheerfulest aspects to her, I fancy. She has had no losses, nor privations; no lack of love, nor necessity of compensation."

"None that I know of," Mrs. Revere assented. "She is an orphan, you know, but her parents died in infancy, and her grandmother idolizes her. She has other relatives, and love and consideration in plenty. Yes, her life has been very happy."

"Yet in all her youth and happiness she seeks religion, and finds it — for that is very evident — her best possession. Inspired by it, she makes a sacrifice of herself, day after day, for a grumbling old man. She runs the risk of offending others whom it would be pleasant for her to please, and finds enjoyment in things that would be a burden if they were not dictated by this all-pervading principle. I do not make it clear to you, perhaps, but like King Agrippa I am tempted sometimes to say to her, My good little girl, almost thou persuadest me to be a Christian."

It would be difficult to describe Mrs. Revere's emotions as she listened to this. She understood him, and thanked God with a full heart for his infinite grace, which in so many diverse ways, by so many different avenues, sought out and reached men's souls. She had no feeling of petty disappointment that it was Evelyn's influence, not hers which had prevailed. She only prayed that the work which his Holy Spirit had begun, through whatever instrument, might be completed and made perfect to his glory.

She went down after a while to look for Evelyn, who had had letters to write that afternoon. Mrs. Hazleton told her that she had gone to the village to post her letters, and had been absent quite long enough to have returned again, unless possibly she had joined some of the young ladies in a walk. Clara Barton and Fanny Rushmore had gone to the bathing-house; Evelyn might be with them.

Mrs. Revere thought she would take a walk herself. She might meet Evelyn, and she felt an unusual longing to talk with her. Not that she meant to tell her what Dr. Gresham had said of her; that would destroy the unconsciousness which added so much to her grace in his eyes.

She walked down nearly to the post-office,

but saw nothing of her; and then came a remembrance of the twins, whom she had not seen for a week, and she turned aside toward the path that led to the cottages by the railroad. Half-way down the hill-side, a little boy ran up to her with an eager cry:

"Please ma'am, will you come to Mrs. Clark's house? Her baby's got a fit, and the young lady that comes with you is there. She sent me to fetch you."

Mrs. Revere quickened her steps. Mrs. Clark was the mother of the twins, and this little fellow was a neighbor's child to whom she had often spoken kindly.

"Are you sure it is Miss Evelyn who is there?" she asked, wondering.

"It's the young lady that comes with you," the child persisted. And Mrs. Revere hurried on, in some anxiety about Evelyn as well as in haste to do what she might for the infant. A wailing cry struck her ear as she entered the cottage. A group of curious children were hanging round the door, and two or three women were in the room itself; but Evelyn's delicate face and figure shone out in striking contrast among them. She was sitting with one of the twins in her lap; the mother was hushing the other at her breast, and crying bitterly herself. The child that Evelyn held was very still, and a gray, pallid look was settling over its little pinched features. Mrs. Revere saw at a glance that it was dead.

"I am so glad you have come!" was Evelyn's tearful exclamation as her friend approached. "This dear little baby—oh! isn't it pitiful?"

Her voice broke; the quivering lips and pale, excited face showed her keen distress, though she struggled to maintain her usual self-control.

"What is the matter?" Mrs. Revere asked, greatly shocked. "They were both so well when I was here last. Why did you not send me word when the child was ill?"

"It was took all of a sudden, ma'am;" the weeping mother checked her sobs to answer. "It only seemed a little dull like, this morning, and I thought it was the hot weather. But when the young lady came a while ago, it was just in a fit. And she took it and put it in warm water and tried to bring it to, but it was gone, in a minute like. It died in her arms, ma'am. God bless her for trying to save it!"

There was nothing to be done but to prepare the little body for its last resting-place; and Evelyn assisted to bathe the tiny limbs, and robe them in one of the little slips which her own hands had made. It was the first time in her life that she had come so close to death; it gave her inexpressible thoughts.

They stayed with the mother till the twilight was gathering, shadowy and dim, around the little shrouded figure. Mrs. Revere talked and prayed with her, and Evelyn felt as if she was lifted above the world, in a holier atmosphere where the Spirit of God was a visible presence.

"How did it happen that you were there?" Mrs. Revere asked, when they went home silently together. "It was a great comfort, but you never told me that you were going to-day."

"I did not know, myself. I went out to post my letters, and then I saw some oranges which I thought would be good for poor old Jane,—you know she is so fond of them,—and so I went on till I came to Mrs. Clark's place. And I knew you would like to hear about the twins, so I went in. But I never dreamed of what would happen; I never shall forget the look that came into that little face when the soul went out!"

She stopped, unable to express the feelings that rose within her, and Mrs. Revere took her hand and clasped it in tender sympathy.

"The first time we walked together," she said softly, "you told me that you had only lived for yourself hitherto. Now I want to tell you how good and great a work you are doing, in the effort you are making to renounce self and live for others. God has blessed you more than you know; and you may thank him, and take courage."

CHAPTER VI.

A NEW HOME.

IT is not often, or to many lives, that great occasions come of testing principle or proving faith. It is in the improvement of the daily small opportunities which occur to all, that the Christian who is in earnest to work for God, to do more then others, is recognized. Evelyn's influence had been felt in the house, from that first Sunday evening when even the people who sneered at piety were moved by her reading, and believed in her sincerity. It had not grown less since, but the contrary.

Her regular church-going with Mrs. Revere was an example that began to be followed.

Miss Haviland joined them one Sunday, with an ingenuous little confession. "You make me ashamed of myself, Evelyn, and I'm going to make an effort to recover my self-respect. May I walk with you, Mrs. Revere? I have made up my mind not to stay from church any longer."

Of course she was welcomed, and the next Sunday Mrs. Maxwell and husband, and Mrs. Barton with two of her daughters, made their appearance on the piazza in church attire, when the bells began to ring. Others followed the example instinctively, — there is so much in mutual attraction! — and the minister who had preached so forcibly to one young heart had the opportunity to reach others also; so more good seed was sown, and its fruits were seen in a tacit agreement to "keep the Sabbath holy" at the Glen; at least to a greater extent than had been known before.

Evelyn was not especially fond of children;

she liked to watch them at a little distance, with a certain enjoyment of their grace and gayety and pretty looks ; but she did not concern herself about them, or care to let them know her, until a word from Mrs. Revere took effect.

"Children are opportunities to me," she said. "One can drop seed in a heart that is won."

And Evelyn saw how the little Delgardos hung about her, and a word from her would make peace in the noisiest contentions of the little Bartons, who were rather turbulent amongst each other. She began to notice them, and by degrees — children are easily attracted — she made herself acquainted with them, their differing tempers and habits, and the quality of the soil for seed-dropping. The Cubans had no mother, and were left most of the day to the care of their nurse, who was a conscientious woman, but common-place and uneducated. She took excellent care of them, as far as she knew how, and their father petted and played with them for half an hour when he came back at night. But it was only from Mrs. Revere — and Evelyn afterwards — that they got something like mother-love and interest: the gentle twilight talk, the reading of little books, and telling of Bible stories, and leading upward of the childish mind to thoughts of God.

Dolorita was afraid of the dark, and it sometimes happened that she was put to bed and left alone when her nurse wanted to spend an evening out. Evelyn heard her crying once, as she passed the door on her way down-stairs to join the usual pleasant gathering on the west piazza. It was, this night, a little more pleasant than usual, for her uncle had brought up some brilliant Japanese lanterns and hung them, as it grew dark, in the boughs of the mountain-ash trees, whose graceful foliage and clusters of green berries were picturesquely illuminated by the shifting light and color. All sorts of fantastic shadows were thrown into the piazza, upon the light dresses and bright faces of the ladies; and a corresponding merriment took possession of the party. They sang old songs, they told quaint stories, they laughed and chattered in innocent and harmonious enjoyment, which Evelyn was sharing to the full. Her aunt sent her up-stairs for a shawl, and it was on her way down again, that she heard Dolorita's sobs smothered under the bed-clothes.

It was an instant impulse, of course, to go in and comfort her; and the cause of the trouble being explained, the determination was equally prompt to give up her own enjoyment and remain with the child. "Don't cry, dear, I will stay with you. Wait one minute till I take this shawl to my aunt, and then I will come back to you," she said, soothingly.

And Dolorita hushed her sobs, and sat up in bed in eager delight, while Evelyn's light feet flew down to the piazza. Mrs. Revere made a place for her, but Evelyn whispered in her ear, "I want to stay up-stairs for a special reason. Please make it right with aunty, if she misses me."

Mrs. Hazleton was in the full tide of animated conversation, and only noticed her niece with a careless "Thank you dear," when the Shetland shawl was wrapped about her. Mrs. Revere's smile, loving and significant, gave her assent, and Evelyn ran away again, although two or three voices called after her importunately. It was something of an effort to resist them, especially as she had spent the afternoon in reading to Dr. Gresham, and felt the need of a little recreation. But there was no sign of sacrifice in her cheerful behavior to the little girl.

"I am not sleepy," Dolorita said. "My

eyes fly open, and I can't be still. Won't you please talk to me, Miss Yale? Tell me a story about something."

And Evelyn answered kindly, "To be sure I will; you shall stay awake as long as you like, and I will tell you stories. Do you know about the ugly duck?"

"No, indeed, but I should like to!"

So Evelyn told her Hans Anderson's pretty story; and then from that, she slipped into Bible stories, and some sweet, serious talk about God and heaven, and the tender Shepherd who laid down his life for his flock, and who, living again in heaven, watches over his little lambs with loving care.

There are very few children who are not interested and tenderly touched by talk like this. Dolorita's heart swelled as she listened and asked questions, and begged to hear it all over again, and promised to try to be good. It might be only a present impression; she might quarrel with Manuelo the next day, or be naughty to nurse just the same,—do not we older ones yield to our temptations in spite of many resolves?—but nevertheless something was left to germinate.

To multiply instances of the little daily occasions for doing good which Evelyn improved, would be to weary, perhaps, the readers of her summer's history, which we must bring to its close. Her acts of charity and devotion and self-denial were all of the simplest—such as fall within every one's sphere to accomplish—and all performed with silent humility; yet they did not fail of their effect. They stamped her Christian character and gave it influence, so that her religion was recognized and respected even by those who had no sympathy with it.

Dr. Gresham was not one of these any longer. The religious impressions first implanted by a pious mother, forgotten afterward through long years of worldliness and skepticism, and now again revived by Evelyn's unconscious agency, were deepening daily through the same gentle influence. He did not know that Evelyn prayed for him nightly, naming him with all her dearest friends; nor did she know how her prayers were being answered, until one day it came upon her suddenly.

He was recovering the use of his limb slowly, was able to sit up all day, and to walk from one room to the other with some assistance, though not yet to go down-stairs. Evelyn had lent him her shoulder to lean upon more than once; it was not a very sturdy one, but the doctor liked to test its willing strength. It was pleasant to him to be led about by this little girl whom he had grown to love with fatherly tenderness. He had been walking to and fro in his sitting-room for a little while one day, and sat down at length to rest, still keeping his hand upon her patient shoulder. Mrs. Revere sat by the window with a book in her hand, not reading but rather watching him; for there was something peculiar in the look with which he regarded Evelyn, and a secret intuition of what he was pondering came to her.

"Do you remember" he asked presently, turning to her, "something that I told you not long since about this little girl here?"

"Very well, indeed," Mrs. Revere answered gently.

"What was it?" Evelyn asked, from the natural impulse, but she too was startled when she looked up to him. His face was working with some strong emotion, his lips trembled, and he could not easily control his voice to speak.

"I told her," he said presently, looking straight into Evelyn's eyes, with a dewy light in his own, "that you had almost persuaded me to be a Christian. Now I tell you, my child, that you have quite and altogether persuaded me. From this time henceforth, so help me God, I will take his vows upon me, and spend the remainder of my life according to this beginning."

"Now, Eva,"— Mrs. Revere dropped her book, and came to the young girl with an irresistible impulse,—"you never can say again that you have done nothing for your Master. You have won a soul to Christ; is not this something to rejoice over all your life?"

Evelyn threw her arms around her with an inexpressible, wondering happiness. "I am so glad! But how have I done it? I?" she repeated, utterly uncomprehending. "It is you he means, you are so good! I have never dared to say a word, to do any thing but pray."

"Have you done that, truly?" Dr. Gresham asked, smiling happily through tears that he was not ashamed of. "I was sure you had prayed for me; I felt it in my heart."

"Yes indeed, always; every night since you were hurt," she answered warmly. "But I didn't think — I didn't dream — oh! it is too much to believe — "

Her voice failed; she hid her face on Mrs. Revere's shoulder and cried irrepressibly; but they were the happiest tears she had ever shed in her life. Whoever has had, in any degree, a similar experience, will need no interpreter for her emotions.

It was a real and earnest conversion with Dr. Gresham, no sudden or evanescent impulse. His long confinement and the near approach to the things of eternity had compelled thought; and Evelyn's influence had won him to an open profession. With all his heart and mind he now accepted the salvation of Christ, and consecrated the remainder of his life to the service of the Master so long neglected.

When it became known in the house — he was not ashamed to let it be known, and could comprehend now the exaltation with which Mrs. Revere sang her favorite hymn — there were comment and wonder, of course, but no sneering. A better and purer sympathy prevailed, and the matter was talked over reverently, even by the most careless ones.

"It's Evelyn Yale's doing," said Fanny Rushmore, in her out-spoken way. "If any body could persuade me to be good, she would be the one, for she's the only real Christian I know."

"Thank you, Fanny," said her mother, with a rather hurt tone. "You make sweeping accusations."

"Oh, mamma, you know what I mean. You're a Christian, of course; so am I; but we're not like Evelyn."

"I wonder what you have to say about Mrs. Revere," said Miss Haviland a little indignantly. "I agree with you that Evelyn is good and sincere, a dear little thing every way; but Mrs Revere is my idea of a true Christian. It is my opinion that she deserves all the credit of Dr. Gresham's change."

"I forgot her," Fanny acknowledged. "She is lovely, but then"—and she unconsciously repeated Dr. Gresham's argument—"she is so much older, and has had trouble and all that, to make her religious. Evelyn is like us, and she makes us all ashamed by the difference."

"How clear you are, and logical!" Mrs. Rushmore laughed.

"Never mind, so long as I know what I mean. I don't expect you to understand me, mamma."

She turned away carelessly,—Miss Fanny was never very respectful to her lady-mamma—and asked Miss Haviland to take a walk with her. It was near the hour for the evening mail; so they decided to walk to the post-office, and collect such letters as might arrive for the inhabitants of the Glen. It was one of the little excitements of the day, the calling for and distributing these letters; and there was generally a little group of expectants on the piazza, waiting the return of the self-appointed mail carriers.

Evelyn was there to-night with Dolorita, who clung to her especially now-a-days, perched upon her knee.

"There come the letters!" cried the child. "Miss Fanny has a handful. Are you going to get any, I wonder?"

"I hope so," said Evelyn. "I want one from my grandmother."

"I wish I had a grandmother," Dolorita chattered; "I have only got papa and Manuelo; nobody else. Do you love your grandmother dearly?"

"Very dearly," Evelyn returned. "I haven't

any papa or any brother, you know, and my grandmamma is the sweetest old lady in the world. Some time, when we all go back to the city, I shall fetch you to see her. She is fond of little girls."

"How nice!" Dolorita clapped her hands. 'I wish we were going to-morrow."

"Perhaps we will," Evelyn said, absently; then recollected herself and laughed. "I am talking nonsense, Dolorita, I was thinking of my letters. Did you bring me one, Fanny?" as Miss Rushmore came up the steps of the piazza.

"Are you an 'expectation' to-night? What's the use of having letters, just for the nuisance of answering them?" asked that young lady.

"It isn't a nuisance to me. Give me my letter."

"Who told you I had any for you?"

"I saw it in your eyes."

"Take it out of my eyes then," said Fanny

mischievously. "You can't get it from my hands till you tell me who wrote it."

"My grandmother," said Evelyn promptly. "Now give it to me, Fanny; don't tease."

"Your grandmother! that's a very nice story," exclaimed Miss Rushmore. "She writes a very masculine hand, then, Miss Eva, that's all I have to say. It doesn't look in the least like a letter from one's grandmother, not in the least."

She tossed the square, handsomely-directed letter over to Evelyn with a bantering laugh, little dreaming what sad tidings for her friend lay under the masculine hand-writing. Evelyn took it with a sense of disappointment; she had an especial longing to hear from her grandmother to-night, and this was only from her guardian, a mere business epistle, probably. She opened it carelessly, but the very first words arrested her attention sharply.

"Your grandmother is suddenly and dangerously ill."

Evelyn did not wait to read more. She crushed the letter in her hands and ran upstairs to her own room. A terrible foreboding seized upon her, and she must find strength in prayer to bear it. On her knees, with the yearning entreaty, — "if it be possible, let this cup pass from me," — she read the whole story, and found that her worst fears were true. Death was at hand, and soon, very soon, she must stand quite orphaned and alone in the world.

There was a knock at her door, and Mrs. Hazleton hurried in, pale and excited; she too had had letters conveying the sad tidings and urging their instant departure.

"You know it all, Eva?" She saw it in her face. "We must go immediately, you know. The next train leaves in half an hour, and you will have only time to change your dress. I have sent for a carriage."

She hurried away to make her own preparations, and Evelyn stood still in a sort of stupor of despair. She felt suddenly crushed and helpless. What would her life be without this nearest and tenderest interest? How could she bear the loss of the only mother-love she had ever known? Why had she left her and lost these last precious weeks?

A soft voice, full of tenderest sympathy, called her. She went mechanically to the door, and Mrs. Revere clasped her with a close, fond embrace.

"My darling! My darling!" she murmured; and the words thrilled Evelyn through all her despair. Mrs. Revere never gave such lightly. "I know what has happened," she said, "and I am praying for you with all my heart. God give you strength and comfort; he can, he will, my precious child!"

Evelyn had no words to answer. She could only sob out her grief upon the loving heart that shared it with a strange sense of sweet ness in this rare tenderness. She had longed for it many a time; it was given to her in all the fullness that her heart could desire.

But there was little time to spare. She had to dress for the journey, and Mrs. Revere packed her traveling-bag with the few necessaries that she could take with her, and made all the little preparations that Evelyn, in her bewilderment, could not think of. Her very presence was strength and soothing to the young girl, so excited with anxious dread and suspense. She wondered how she could have endured that hour without it.

There was brief time for leave-taking, but Evelyn flew up to Dr. Gresham's room and got his fervent "God bless you;" and the whole household gathered round her as she went down to the carriage, with kind expressions of sympathy and earnest wishes that the trouble might be averted. Fanny Rushmore kissed her with a sort of passionate pity, not able to speak for real feeling; and little Dolorita clung to her, crying, till the child had to be taken away. But Mrs. Revere's kiss was the last upon her lips, and her whispered words, "Remember, whatever happens, next to God, you belong to me," lingered in her heart all the way, and brought a sense of comfort and love still left to her, in the midst of all her grief.

Three days later, the tale of life was told, and Evelyn's bereavement was complete. She had come in time for many last sweet words and deeds; her grandmother died with love and blessing for her, — the last articulate sounds upon her lips. Now in her place lay a white image, cold and awful in rigid stillness; and the orphan girl wept alone with the desolation that motherless children feel. She had never missed her own mother; all her life had been shielded and satisfied by this love which was now taken from her; and its loss was the first real grief she had ever known.

The world seemed very empty to her, sitting alone here with the shrouded figure in the chamber of death below. She would have a home with her uncle, and be properly cared for, of course; but there was little sympathy between Mrs. Hazleton and herself; she would have to live within herself, and learn to do without the constant tenderness, the sympathy with every feeling, the indulgent comprehension, which had been part of her existence before. She was not faithless or despairing; she did not rebel against God who had done this thing. She bent her heart to his will, instead, and prayed humbly and patiently that she might do and bear it in all meekness. Nevertheless, sorrow and loneliness can not be set aside, even when accepted as God's gift. There would be no grace in resignation if the loss was not felt; and Evelyn could not help feeling the sharpness of hers.

The memory of Mrs. Revere's parting words

— it seemed an age since they had been spoken — came back to her with a wistful longing. "If I truly did belong to her!" was the unuttered yearning; and a swift vision of what her life might be — guided, governed, directed in good works and charity by a nature so elevated — flashed before her imagination. Was it a premonition of what would be?

As if soul had answered to soul, Mrs. Revere came, then and there.

The same light tap at her door, the same soft voice which had called to her in her first trouble, three days ago, gave warning now of the earthly presence that she most longed for; and once more Evelyn lay folded to the true heart that beat for her with almost mother-love.

"I could not stay away from you, my child, I could not leave you alone in your sorrow," was the tender greeting. "Do not you belong to me now more than to any one else? Something tells me that it is so, and that you will be given to me soon."

She needed no other response than the close embrace with which Evelyn clung to her, as a child who has found its mother truly; and her already formed resolve was put into action at the earliest moment afterwards.

It did not meet with any determined opposition. Mrs. Hazleton was fond of her husband's niece, and perfectly willing "to do her duty by her," as she would have said. But she was also fond of her ease, and not anxious to assume any responsibilities that might as well be avoided. It was an honor not to be despised, moreover, that a person of Mrs. Revere's influence and position should wish to adopt Evelyn. It implied future social advantages for herself, and was well worthy of consideration.

So, being considered duly, it ended as Mrs.

Revere and Evelyn wished it; and the childless mother took the motherless girl to her own home, as she had taken her to her heart long ago.

Her story for us ends here; but for her begins a new life, happy and beautiful and good beyond that of many; not a life of mere grace and refinement, and returning love for love,—for "if ye salute your brethren only, what do ye more than others?" but one whose object and effort is to fulfill the law of Christ by bearing the burden of others, and in all things to "glorify her Father which is in heaven."

Illustrated Stories for Young Folks.

Young Folks' Cyclopedia of Stories. Quarto, cloth, 3.00.
Contains in one large book the following stories with many illustrations: Five Little Peppers, Two Young Homesteaders, Royal Lowrie's Last Year at St. Olaves, The Dogberry Bunch, Young Rick, Nan the New-Fashioned Girl, Good-for-Nothing Polly and The Cooking Club of Tu-Whit Hollow.

What the Seven Did; or, the Doings of the Wordsworth Club. By Margaret Sidney. Quarto, boards, 1.75.
The Seven are little girl neighbors who meet once a week at their several homes. They helped others and improved themselves.

Me and My Dolls. By L. T. Meade. Quarto, 50 cts.
A family history. Some of the dolls have had queer adventures. Twelve full-page illustrations by Margaret Johnson.

Little Wanderers in Bo-Peep's World. Quarto, boards, double lithograph covers, 50 cts.

Polly and the Children. By Margaret Sidney. Boards, quarto, 50 cts.
The story of a funny parrot and two charming children. The parrot has surprising adventures at the children's party and wears a medal after the fire.

Five Little Peppers. By Margaret Sidney. 12mo, 1.50.
Story of five little children of a fond, faithful and capable "mamsie." Full of young life and family talk.

Seal Series. 10 vols., boards, double lithographed covers, quarto.
Rocky Fork, Old Caravan Days, The Dogberry Bunch, by Mary H. Catherwood; The Story of Honor Bright and Royal Lowrie's Last Year at St. Olaves, by Charles R. Talbot; Their Club and Ours, by John Preston True; From the Hudson to the Neva, by David Ker; The Silver City, by Fred A. Ober; Two Young Homesteaders, by Theodora Jenness; The Cooking Club of Tu-whit Hollow, by Ella Farman.

Cats' Arabian Nights. By Abby Morton Diaz. Quarto, cloth, 1.75; boards, 1.25.
The wonderful cat story of cat stories told by Pussyanita that saved the lives of all the cats.

Science Stories.

My Wonder Story. By Anne K. Benedict. Quarto, illustrated, cloth, 1.50.

A young folks' science story based on physiology. A high-school teacher writes: "One might well wish himself a little child again to be charmed with this study of his own body. No 'dry bones' here."

Look-About Club. By Mary E. Bamford. Quarto, boards, 1.25.

The club is a family given to the study of animal life. Under the guise of play they learn about the folks in the brook, on the ground and in the air.

My Land and Water Friends. By Mary E. Bamford. Seventy illustrations by Bridgman. Boards, 1.25.

An out-door book giving delicious little accounts of strange and familiar creatures. The book is a treat for children under ten.

Overhead. By Annie Moore and Laura D. Nichols. Quarto, boards, 1.25.

A trip to the moon, Saturn, the sun and various other stations with a bit of easy astronomy sprinkled in.

Underfoot. By Laura D. Nichols. Quarto, boards, 1.25.

Peeps into the earth we live on, especially at its caves, volcanoes, fossils and petrifactions.

Up Hill and Down Dale. By Laura D. Nichols. Quarto, boards, 1.25.

A story of nature. Juvenile readers will be very much pleased with little Nelly Marlow and her life at Hickory Corners.

Eyes Right. By Adam Stwin. Quarto, boards, 1.25.

A little fellow with an eager, exploring soul back of his eyes; to make them see is the author's delight, and he loves both a good romp and a quiet talk with the boys.

Nelly Marlow in Washington. By Laura D. Nichols. Quarto, boards, 1.25.

Nelly goes to Washington and takes her friends along and ends in the Adirondacks. She learns history at one place and natural nce at the other.

Young Folks' Illustrated Quartos.

Wide Awake Volume Z. Quarto, boards, 1.75.
Good literature and art have been put into this volume. Henry Bacon's paper about Rosa Bonheur, the great painter of horses and lions, and Steffeck's painting of Queen Louise with Kaiser William would do credit to any Art publication.

Chit Chat for Boys and Girls. Quarto, boards, 75 cts.
A volume of selected pieces upon every conceivable subject. As a distinctive feature it devotes considerable space to Home Life and Sports and Pastimes.

Good Cheer for Boys and Girls.
Short stories, sketches, poems, bits of history, biography and natural history.

Our Little Men and Women for 1888. Quarto, boards, 1.50.
No boys and girls who have this book can be ignorant beyond their years of history, natural history, foreign sights or the good times of other boys and girls.

Babyland for 1888. Quarto, boards, 75 cts.
Finger-plays, cricket stories, Tales told by a Cat and scores of jingles and pictures. Large print and easy words. Colored frontispiece.

Kings and Queens at Home. By Frances A. Humphrey. Quarto, boards, 50 cts.
Short-story accounts of living royal personages.

Queen Victoria at Home. By Frances A. Humphrey. Quarto, boards, 50 cts.
Pen picture of a noble woman. It will aid in educating the heart by presenting the domestic side of the queen's character.

Stories about Favorite Authors. By Frances A. Humphrey. Quarto, boards, 50 cts.
Little literature lessons for little boys and girls.

Child Lore. Edited by Clara Doty Bates. Quarto, cloth, tinted edges, 2.25; boards, 1.50.
More than 50,000 copies sold. The most successful quarto for children.

Helpful Books for Young Folks.

Danger Signals. By Rev. F. E. Clark, President of the United Society of Christian Endeavor. 12mo, cloth, 75 cts.
The enemies of youth from the business man's standpoint. The substance of a series of addresses delivered two or three years ago in one of the Boston churches.

Marion Harland's Cookery for Beginners. 12mo, vellum cloth, 75 cts.
The untrained housekeeper needs such directions as will not confuse and discourage her. Marion Harland makes her book simple and practical enough to meet this demand.

Bible Stories. By Laurie Loring. 4to, boards, 35 cts.
Very short stories with pictures. The Creation, Noah and the Dove, Samuel, Joseph, Elijah, the Christ Child, the Good Shepherd, Peter, etc.

The Magic Pear. Oblong, 8vo, boards, 75 cts.
Twelve outline drawing lessons with directions for the amusement of little folks. They are genuine pencil puzzles for untaught fingers. A pear gives shape to a dozen animal pictures.

What O'Clock Jingles. By Margaret Johnson. Oblong, 8vo, boards, 75 cts.
Twelve little counting lessons. Pretty rhymes for small children. Twenty-seven artistic illustrations by the author.

Ways for Boys to Make and Do Things. 60 cts.
Eight papers by as many different authors, on subjects that interest boys. A book to delight active boys and to inspire lazy ones.

Our Young Folks at Home. 4to, boards, 1.00.
A collection of illustrated prose stories by American authors and artists. It is sure to make friends among children of all ages. Colored frontispiece.

Peep of Day Series. 3 vols., 1.20 each.
Peep of Day, Line upon Line, Precept upon Precept. Sermonettes for the children, so cleverly preached that the children will not grow sleepy.

Home Primer. Boards, square, 8vo, 50 cts.
A book for the little ones to learn to read in before they are old enough to be sent off to school. 100 illustrations.

Natural History.

Stories and Pictures of Wild Animals. By Anna F. Burnham. Quarto, boards, 75 cts.

Big letters, big pictures and easy stories of elephants, lions, tigers, lynxes, jaguars, bears and many others.

Life and Habits of Wild Animals. Quarto, cloth, 1.50.

The very best book young folks can have if they are at all interested in Natural History. If they are not yet interested it will make them so. Illustrated from designs by Joseph Wolf.

Children's Out-Door Neighbors. By Mrs. A. E. Andersen-Maskell. 3 volumes, 12mo, cloth, each 1.00.

Three instructive and interesting books: Children with Animals, Children with Birds, Children with Fishes. The author has the happy faculty of interesting boys and girls in the wonderful neighbors around them and that without introducing anything which is not borne out by the knowledge of learned men.

Some Animal Pets. By Mrs. Oliver Howard. Quarto, boards, 35 cts.

The experiences of a Colorado family with young, wild and tame animals. It is one of the pleasantest animal books we have met in many a day. Well thought, well written, well pictured, the book itself, apart from its contents, is attractive. Full page pictures.

Tiny Folk in Red and Black. Quarto, boards, 35 cts.

The tiny folk are ants and they make as interesting a study as human folk — perhaps more interesting in the opinion of some. The book gives a full and graphic description of their many wise and curious ways — how they work, how they harvest their grain, how they milk their cows, etc. It will teach the children to keep eyes and ears open.

My Land and Water Friends. By Mary E. Bamford. Seventy illustrations by Bridgman. Quarto, cloth, 1.50.

The frog opens the book with a "talk" about himself, in the course of which he tells us all about the changes through which he passes before he arrives at perfect froghood. Then the grasshopper talks and is followed by others, each giving his view of life from his own individual standpoint.

www.ingramcontent.com/pod-product-compliance
Lightning Source LLC
LaVergne TN
LVHW021418110826
845150LV00007B/1980

* 9 7 8 1 4 2 5 5 0 9 4 7 7 *